Zack
at the
Dentist

For Aaron & Sean & Dr. Ford
—J.L.

To Lynn & Zack
—J.M.

Library of Congress Cataloging-in-Publication Data

London, Jonathan, 1947-
Zack at the dentist / by Jonathan London ; illustrated by Jack Medoff.
p. cm.
Summary: Zack the chimpanzee goes to the dentist to see about his toothache.
ISBN 0-439-53776-2
[1. Dentists—Fiction. 2. Chimpanzees—Fiction. 3. Hippopotamus—Fiction.] I. Medoff, Jack, ill. II. Title.
PZ7.L8432Zac 2004
[E]—dc21   2002155200

10 9 8 7 6 5 4 3   06 07 08

Printed in the U.S.A. 23
First printing, January 2004

Zack at the Dentist

by Jonathan London
Illustrated by Jack Medoff

Cartwheel
·B·O·O·K·S·®

SCHOLASTIC INC.

New York   Toronto   London   Auckland   Sydney   Mexico City
New Delhi   Hong Kong   Buenos Aires

"Zack!" said Mom.
"It's time to go to
the dentist!"

"I don't *want* to go to the dentist!" said Zack.
"But you *need* to go to the dentist!" said Mom.
"You said you had a toothache!"

"Only when I'm awake!" said Zack.
And Zack shut his eyes and
pretended to snore.

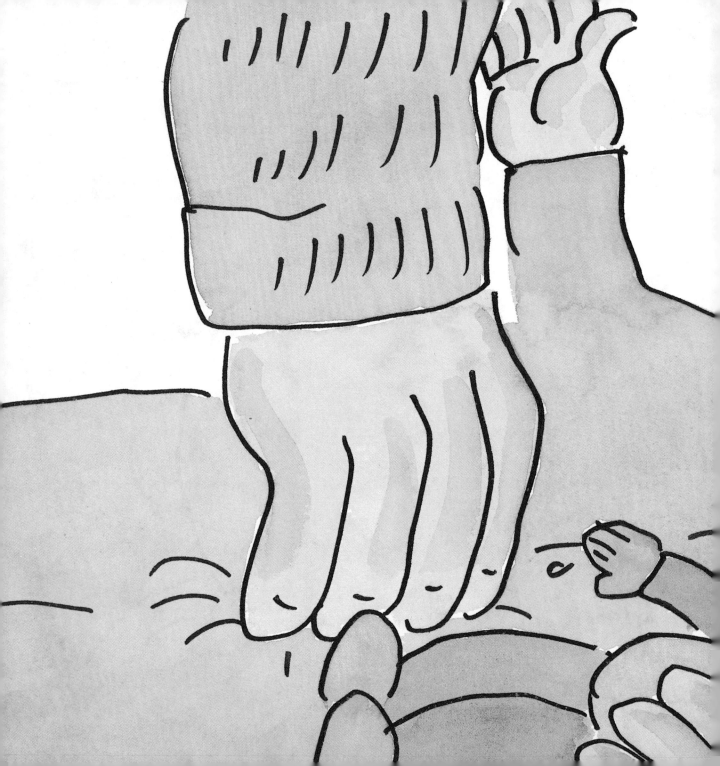

"Wake up, Goofus!" said Mom.
And she tickled Zack
till he giggled with glee.

"Okay," said Zack, "I'll go."
"Not till you brush your teeth,"
said Mom.
So Zack brushed his teeth—
brusha, brusha, brusha.

"Did you use any toothpaste?"
asked Mom
"Yep!" Zack lied.
"Let's go, then," said Mom.

"Wait!" said Zack. "I'm hungry.
I wanna banana!"
"But you already brushed!"
cried Mom.
"So? I'll brush again!"
So Zack ate a banana . . .

then went to brush his teeth
again—this time with toothpaste.
He squeezed the tube in his fist—
but it squirted all over the mirror!
"Whoopsy!"
So Zack didn't brush at all.

Then he stuck a banana in his pocket,
and off they went to the dentist,
hand in hand.

At the dentist, they had to wait.
"*Owww!*" moaned Zack. "My tooth hurts!
I want to go home and go to bed!" he said.
"Poor baby," said Mom.

Zack swung his feet—
and his shoe flew off
and hit the receptionist
in the head—*bingo*!

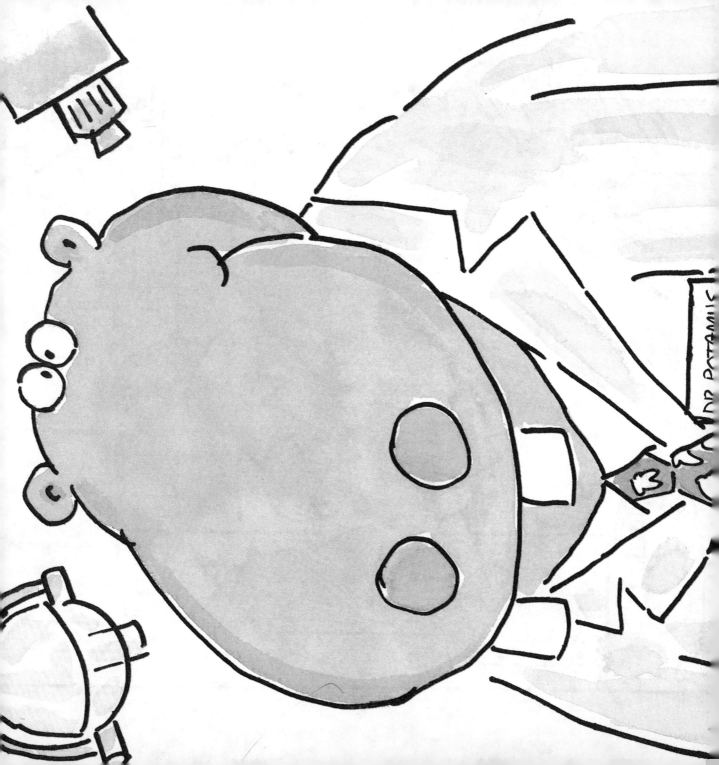

At last, Dr. Potamus came and led Zack to the dentist's chair.

The dentist smiled and said,
"Open your mouth and
we'll have a look."

Zack opened his mouth—and his breath
almost knocked Dr. Potamus over.
"Ugh!" he cried. "Banana breath!"
"Whoopsy!" said Zack.

Dr. Potamus took X ray's of Zack's teeth.

Zack had to wait some more. So he picked up a plastic model of a set of teeth and stuck it in his mouth.

When Dr. Potamus came back,
Zack smiled.
Dr. Potamus almost fainted.

"Time to drill your cavity,"
said Dr. Potamus.
"Oh, no!" cried Zack.

"But first—" said Dr. Potamus,
"a shot of novocaine."
"Oh, no!" cried Zack—
and *he* almost fainted.
But luckily, Zack only felt a tiny sting.
Then his gums got all numb—
even his lips got numb.
They felt like rubber.

And when Dr. Potamus drilled, Zack heard it more than he felt it. And he stared into the bright light overhead and imagined he was on a beach in the hot sun.

"All done!" said Dr. Potamus. "But you'll need
to come back to have your teeth cleaned."
"I brush my teeth!" cried Zack.
"Well," said Dr. Potamus, "if I were grading, I'd give
you a D for brushing and an F for flossing…

but I'd give you an A for smiling!"
And Zack grinned from ear to ear.

"Wanna banana?" asked Zack.
He pulled the banana out of his pocket.
It was getting kind of mushy.
"No, thanks!" said Dr. Potamus.

"But here's a new toothbrush for you."
Zack stuck the toothbrush in his pocket,
hopped out of the chair, and peeled the
banana as he left.

"How was it, Zack?" asked Mom.
"Cool!" said Zack.
"Dr. Potamus gave me
an A for smiling! And
my toothache's gone!"

Suddenly, there was a big THUD!
"What was that?" said Mom.
"Whoopsy!" said Zack.
"I think Dr. Potamus had
an accident."

Back at home, Zack made his grade-A smile
in the bathroom mirror.
He liked Dr. Potamus—
but he wasn't in a hurry to go back.

So he brushed his teeth
with his new toothbrush—
brusha, brusha, brusha.
And this time…

he used lots and lots of toothpaste.
"Whoopsy!"
He got a little on his shirt.